Marie-Claire
ANGELS IN WINTER

KATHY STINSON

**Look for the other Marie-Claire stories
in Our Canadian Girl**

Book One: Dark Spring

Book Two: A Season of Sorrow

Book Three: Visitors

Marie-Claire
Angels in Winter

Kathy Stinson

PENGUIN
CANADA

PENGUIN CANADA

Published by the Penguin Group

Penguin Group (Canada), 10 Alcorn Avenue, Toronto, Ontario, Canada M4V 3B2
(a division of Pearson Penguin Canada Inc.)

Penguin Group (USA) Inc., 375 Hudson Street, New York, New York 10014, U.S.A.
Penguin Books Ltd, 80 Strand, London WC2R 0RL, England
Penguin Ireland, 25 St Stephen's Green, Dublin 2, Ireland (a division of Penguin Books Ltd)
Penguin Group (Australia), 250 Camberwell Road, Camberwell, Victoria 3124, Australia
(a division of Pearson Australia Group Pty Ltd)
Penguin Books India Pvt Ltd, 11 Community Centre, Panchsheel Park, New Delhi – 110 017, India
Penguin Group (NZ), Cnr Airborne and Rosedale Roads, Albany, Auckland, New Zealand
(a division of Pearson New Zealand Ltd)
Penguin Books (South Africa) (Pty) Ltd, 24 Sturdee Avenue, Rosebank, Johannesburg 2196,
South Africa

Penguin Books Ltd, Registered Offices: 80 Strand, London WC2R 0RL, England

First published 2004

1 2 3 4 5 6 7 8 9 10   (WEB)

Copyright © Kathy Stinson, 2004
Cover and full-page interior illustrations © Sharif Tarabay, 2004
Chapter-opener illustrations © Janet Wilson, 2004
Design: Matthews Communications Design Inc.
Map © Sharon Matthews

*Publisher's note: This book is a work of fiction. Names, characters, places and incidents either
are the product of the author's imagination or are used fictitiously, and any resemblance
to actual persons living or dead, events, or locales is entirely coincidental.*

Manufactured in Canada.

LIBRARY AND ARCHIVES CANADA CATALOGUING IN PUBLICATION

Stinson, Kathy
Marie-Claire : angels in winter / Kathy Stinson.

(Our Canadian girl)
"Marie-Claire, book four".
ISBN 0-14-301673-3

I. Title. II. Title: Angels in winter. III. Series.

PS8587.T56M383 2004   jC813'.54   C2004-903062-0

Visit the Penguin Group (Canada) website at **www.penguin.ca**

To the key "Canadian girls"
in my life: my daughter, Kelly;
my daughter-in-law, Antonella;
my stepdaughters, Stephanie and Kate;
and my granddaughter, Claire

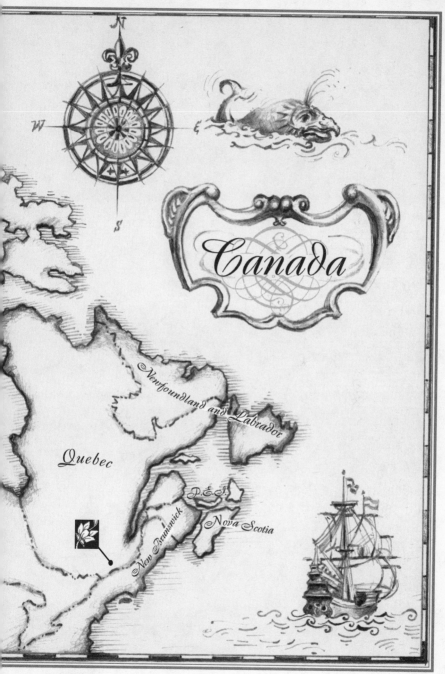

Canada

Newfoundland and Labrador

Quebec

P.E.I.

New Brunswick

Nova Scotia

 Marks the location of the story

CHRISTMASTIME IN MARIE-CLAIRE'S MONTREAL

I N 1885, church steeples dominate the skyline of Montreal. They soar high above the homes and commercial buildings in both English and French parts of the city, in wealthy neighbourhoods and in poor. In the lives of most families, religion plays an important part. It is the basis for community and offers comfort in times of sorrow. It also offers cause for celebration. In the Christian churches, Christmas marks the birth of Christ and is an especially celebratory time.

In families like Marie-Claire's, the focus of Christmas is very much on special masses that celebrate the birth of *l'Enfant Jésus* and on gatherings of family and friends, during which there is abundant food and merriment. These gatherings can last for days. Any gifts exchanged are modest and are generally given only to the youngest children. Exchange of gifts among older family members is more likely to take place at New Year's.

Christmas is also a celebration of the birth of Christ in families like Laura's, the wealthy English girl whom Marie-Claire met following her encounter with a runaway horse. Their Christmas celebrations differ in some ways, however, as does much about their day-to-day lives.

Family ties are strong in Montreal, and people will go to considerable effort to come together at this time. This is the first year in Canada's history that it is possible for people to travel by train to and from the country's westernmost province. For Marie-Claire, the significance of the national railway lies in the fact that her beloved Tante Thérèse and Oncle Henri, who have done well for themselves in Toronto, are coming by train to celebrate Christmas. They will bring with them Marie-Claire's new cousin, Angélique.

CHAPTER № 1

Marie-Claire hugged her nightgown against her skin as she scampered down the stairs to the outhouse in the back lane. It was the warmest nightgown she had ever owned, but the wind still crept inside it and curled around her legs and neck. She should have taken time to grab the shawl from its hook by the door.

Inside the small wooden shack, Marie-Claire was protected from the wind and stopped shivering for long enough to lift her nightgown and do her business. But she was certainly not as warm as she had been when using the toilet inside the wealthy English girl's house. There the toilet sat in a special room with a bathtub and a sink, both with their taps full of warm water. In the outhouse, the wind found its way through cracks between the boards. As soon and as quickly as she could, Marie-Claire skittered across the frozen laneway, back to the house.

Maman had been up for some time and had already lit the fire. After warming herself at the wood stove, Marie-Claire pulled on her grey woollen dress. She thought again of Laura and wondered which of the many pretty dresses in her closet she would be wearing today. Staying at Laura's home, after her run-in with the Waterfords' horse, had been like visiting a different country. So large were the rooms, so luxurious the indoor plumbing. So many beautiful *things* there were everywhere—like the angel on the tree that Marie-Claire had glimpsed for only a moment.

"Can we get a Christmas tree this year, Maman?" Marie-Claire asked.

Maman laughed and tossed a slice of bread into the sizzling pan.

Marie-Claire wondered what Laura was doing now. Giving away her lovely nightgown had been very generous. Marie-Claire wished she could give Laura something in return. A Christmas present. But what?

She thought about it all day at school but still had no idea as Sister Chantal waved the girls out the door. *"Au revoir,"* the nun called out. *"Joyeux Noël."* There would be no more school now until January. No more adding and subtracting— too bad. No more memory work—*hourra!*

Without stopping to think about why she was not going home, Marie-Claire headed across the city instead of down the hill to her own street. Snow had fallen throughout the day, and many horses were now pulling sleighs instead of carriages. Marie-Claire kept well clear of their path. When she remembered how the Waterford horse had descended upon her, her heart still beat fast!

Perhaps, she thought, if she got more than one candy at New Year's, she could take Laura a piece. Marie-Claire skidded across an ice rink, her injured wrist tucked carefully inside her coat. As she zipped along, she dodged the people on real skates. Laura probably had real skates.

And Laura would probably receive lots of candy herself.

Starting up the hill, Marie-Claire slowed her steps. Everyone now was speaking English. The houses were large and so very far apart. How oddly out of place she felt in this neighbourhood, and yet at the same time she felt drawn to it.

Maybe a clothespin doll like the one she had made for Emilie last spring would make a nice present for Laura. Emilie had certainly loved hers.

But then, Emilie had been much younger than Laura and had never seen a doll like the one in Laura's room.

In front of Laura's house, Marie-Claire stopped. If she had a gift with her, she could knock on the door right now. Perhaps she would be invited inside. Perhaps Laura would ask her to stay and play. Behind which of the many windows were Laura's bedroom and her doll and her snow globe?

As she tried to figure it out, the front door opened. Wearing fancy hats and coats, Laura's parents stepped out to the fine carriage awaiting them.

Marie-Claire turned away and began to run.

What would a girl who owned a doll with real hair, a red silk dress, stockings, and shoes want with a clothespin dressed in a scrap of cloth? Marie-Claire ran until she had a stitch in her side, then kept on running. There was nothing a *poor little French girl* could give to a girl like Laura. Oh, how those words still stung.

Comfortably back near her own home, Marie-Claire slowed down to catch her breath. On only a few houses did she see the awful black-and-yellow SMALLPOX/LA PICOTTE notices that had hung in so many places through the summer and fall. It seemed, as Louis said, that the epidemic was almost over.

By the side of a church, as she walked along, Marie-Claire spotted a patch of untrampled snow. She looked around to make sure no nuns were nearby. What she was about to do, they would consider most unladylike.

Marie-Claire stepped from the walkway onto the fresh snow. Carefully, she turned and lay down flat on her back. So cold it was, the snow on her neck and on the bare wrist of her good arm. But after her long run, she didn't mind a bit. She gazed up at the blue sky that seemed to suggest anything was possible. Together and apart, together and apart, Marie-Claire swished her legs, at the same time sliding one arm up and down through the snow till her limbs tingled.

She stood up, brushed the snow from her clothing as best she could, and turned to admire her *étoile de mer*. Her starfish in the snow looked, she thought, rather like a lopsided angel. It reminded her of the angel on the tree at Laura's house.

There must be *something* nice she could give to Laura. If only she could think what it would be.

CHAPTER 2

The next day Maman removed the splint from Marie-Claire's injured wrist. How wonderful it felt to swing her arm freely. Except for when she tried to bend her wrist too far, it didn't hurt at all now.

In preparation for the arrival of Tante Thérèse and Oncle Henri with their new baby, Marie-Claire polished the table while Maman took the braided rugs outside and shook them. She and Maman baked extra biscuits and readied the cradle for Angélique.

How lovely it would be to have a baby in the

house again. Of all the Linteau family who had stayed with the Laroches after their house had burned down, Marie-Claire missed Michel the most.

And yet, as she well knew, a baby's life could be so fragile. As if able to read her daughter's mind, Maman said, "Tante Thérèse writes in her letters that Angélique is a strong and healthy girl."

Marie-Claire was smoothing the cradle blanket in place when there was a knock at the door.

"Are they here yet?" It was her cousin Lucille and her little sister, Bernadette.

"Not yet," said Maman. "In fact, Marie-Claire, if you'd like to play outside before you go to meet their train, there is time."

Marie-Claire scrambled into her coat, and the girls took turns jumping from the steps into the growing piles of snow in the alleyway below.

"I was hoping," Lucille said, "that the Linteau family might stay with you a little longer."

"You were?"

"*Oui!* Then perhaps Tante Thérèse would come and stay at our house instead of at yours."

"Ah, but she is my maman's sister, *non?*"

"And my papa's sister also."

"Oh, but a brother and a sister is not the same thing as a sister and a sister."

"No," Lucille said, waiting for Bernadette to roll out of the way before jumping down into the snowbank, "but I wish I had a brother all the same."

"Yes, I am very lucky to have Louis." Marie-Claire did not say how much she wished she still had a sister.

Back up the steps she and her cousins ran. They jumped down again many times before Louis came out and said it was time to go to the train station. Lucille and Bernadette headed home.

Louis and Marie-Claire walked through the streets as quickly as the accumulating snow would allow, chatting along the way about the arrival of their relatives, about Céleste and when Louis would see her again, and about Marie-Claire's wish to give Laura a gift.

"You have been very busy knitting that scarf for Papa," Louis said. "Is there something you could make for this girl Laura?"

"I don't know. It is only a few days now until Christmas."

On one corner, a group of carollers stood singing. On another a street hawker cried out, "Tinware? Anyone with tinware to mend?"

A woman whose pot had a split handle came out of a nearby house. Marie-Claire joined a group of children gathered around the tinsmith's charcoal fire. She loved to watch him as he perched on his box, repairing things with his soldering iron and resin.

"You cannot watch for long this time, Marie-Claire," Louis said. "The train will soon be arriving."

Outside the station stood several horses, sleighs, and carriages. On the platform, many people were waiting for the train. So many people, coming or going.

"Just think," Louis said, "soon it will be possible to get on a train here in Montreal and travel clear across Canada to British Columbia."

To Marie-Claire, the city of Toronto, where Tante Thérèse and Oncle Henri lived now, seemed a whole world away. More country beyond that, she could hardly begin to imagine.

From far down the tracks came the long whistle of the train. Everyone turned in the direction from which it was coming. The ground beneath the platform began to vibrate. The whistle blew again, much louder and closer this time. Along with the rumble came the sound of what seemed to be a huge animal, breathing wheezily.

The monstrous bulk of the train soon filled the station. Its huge wheels and the long steel arms that moved with them chugged hypnotically along—slowing, slowly slowing, slower—mesmerizing Marie-Claire with their motion.

At last the train hissed to a stop, and Marie-Claire realized how tightly she had been clinging to her brother's arm. What would it be like, she wondered, to ride up inside this steel monster, high above the tracks and the world outside?

"Look! Here they are!"

Marie-Claire could not see her aunt and uncle among the crush of people but ran along behind Louis, holding tightly to the tail of his coat. Among the crowds of travellers and greeters, they called out, "Tante Thérèse! Oncle Henri!" then exchanged hugs and exclamations of delight at finding one another so quickly.

"How you have grown, Louis!" Tante Thérèse said. "You have become a man!"

Louis blushed but held himself tall.

"And how about this young lady?" Oncle Henri said. "She is even more beautiful than she was when we left for Toronto. Tell me, Marie-Claire, how is your maman doing now—and your papa?"

Allowing themselves to be swept out of the station with the moving crowds, they had little chance to look at the new baby, bundled and held close against Tante Thérèse's coat.

"Shall we take the streetcar back?" Louis suggested. "It is a long way to carry a baby and a suitcase, but I am not yet a rich enough man to suggest a cab ride."

Everyone laughed and agreed that a streetcar ride would be quite luxurious enough.

Settled in their seats, Tante Thérèse said to Marie-Claire, "Would you like to hold the baby?"

Angélique felt heavier than Marie-Claire expected her to. She had the cutest little button of a nose and her pink eyelids quivered. After all the commotion at the station, Marie-Claire could hardly believe the baby was still sleeping.

Riding the streetcar as it jerked along proved not much faster than walking. It made many stops, wherever passengers called out to be picked up or let off. Also, the snow was now drifting in huge piles, and the driver had to keep on stopping to wait while men with shovels dug out sections of track. Darkness began to fall over the city.

Papa would be out now with other firemen, each of them lighting the gas lamps in the streets near their fire stations. With the coming of night, the air grew colder, but with straw on the floor and horse blankets spread on their laps, Marie-Claire and the other riders were very comfortable on the streetcar. Just the same, when it again had to stop so that men could clear the track of snow, someone on the wooden bench behind Marie-Claire said they'd better soon replace the cars on this line with sleighs, as had already been done on the hillier north–south lines in the city.

With Angélique sleeping contentedly in her arms, Marie-Claire didn't mind how long the ride took. She felt already as if she had known this baby forever. As her aunt, uncle, and brother chatted about plans for the visit, Marie-Claire wished that Emilie could have met this lovely baby whose name was like the angels she had so adored.

In front of the church where they had to get off the streetcar, in the dim light cast by the gas lamps, a statue of an angel with outstretched wings watched protectively over a carved nativity scene. The Virgin Mary, with Josèph at her side, held *l'Enfant Jésus* in her arms. Snow settled lightly on the curve of the angel's wings.

In that moment, Marie-Claire knew what she would give to Laura.

CHAPTER № 3

"*We want to get off here,*" *Louis said to* the streetcar driver. The man pulled the reins, the horses stopped, and Marie-Claire passed Angélique back to Tante Thérèse.

The temperature fell as they walked the rest of the way home, but a cozy room and the smell of stew and fresh biscuits awaited them.

After supper, Tante Thérèse was quietly nursing Angélique in the corner, Maman was doing some mending, and the men were taking turns at arm-wrestling. "Maman," Marie-Claire said, "may I please use a block of soap to make something?"

Maman had an extra on the shelf in the pantry, Marie-Claire was sure.

"Are you planning to carve something?"

"Yes, but don't worry. I will be careful with the knife."

"I know you will. What are you planning to make?"

"An angel," Marie-Claire answered. She hesitated before adding, "For the English girl who gave me her nightgown."

"Oh? And how are you planning to get it to her?"

"I ... I suppose I will take it to her."

Maman snipped off the wool with which she had been mending Papa's sock. "Ah, so you want an excuse to go back there, do you? Now that you have had a little taste of the fine comforts of the wealthy?"

Marie-Claire opened her mouth to argue, but the hard truth was that she did want to go back. She did want another taste of the luxuries in the Waterfords' mansion.

"You may have half a block of the soap," Maman said. "And please collect the bits and shavings as you work. Even small ones will be useful."

Louis cut the block of soap in half, and Marie-Claire settled near the wood stove to begin scraping. She had never carved soap before but had seen others do it. It didn't look any harder than cleaning fish, and she was very good at that now. She would save doing the wings until last, she decided, when she was used to the feel of how the knife and the soap worked together. She would start with the shape of the angel's skirt.

Tante Thérèse raised Angélique to her shoulder. "Who is the English girl you are making this for?" she asked.

By the time the whole story of Marie-Claire's encounter with the runaway horse and her stay at the mansion on the hill was told, the angel had a skirt and a head. Marie-Claire had forgotten to leave enough soap at the top for a halo but hoped she could solve that problem when the rest of the carving was finished.

When everyone began getting ready for bed, Marie-Claire begged to be allowed to stay up. "I have just one more wing to do. See?" With her hand around the chunk of uncarved wing, she held up the angel that was, almost magically it seemed, emerging from the block of soap.

"Isn't it beautiful," Tante Thérèse said. "I hope this Laura will appreciate what you are doing."

"She will," Marie-Claire said.

"Remember," Maman said, "how Emilie loved to hear stories about angels? She would have loved a little angel like that, wouldn't she?"

There was a moment's silence in the room as everyone paused to think of the little girl now with the angels in heaven. Then everyone said *bonne nuit* and left Marie-Claire with one burning candle by which to finish her soap angel.

It was hard getting the second wing to match the first. Rather than risk breaking it off by over-working it, Marie-Claire decided to leave one wing a little thicker than the other. She tried to fashion a halo for the angel from the scrapings, but in the end carved away a little of her hair instead, leaving only a slight suggestion of a halo.

By the time the angel was finished, the fire in the wood stove had gone out.

"Please, God," Marie-Claire whispered, holding the finished soap angel in the palm of her hand, "I hope you are taking excellent care of my little sister."

She shivered as she stepped into her nightgown. She blew out the candle and slipped quickly beneath her grey blanket, beside Tante Thérèse who was already asleep. In the cradle Angélique was making snuffling sounds. In different parts of the room, Louis and Oncle Henri were snoring in unison.

Marie-Claire shifted in her bed. Her nightgown was soft and warm against her skin. As she slept, angels swirled in her dreams. In the middle of them all stood Emilie, cupping the soap angel gently in her hands.

CHAPTER N°. 4

How strange it was to awake to the sound of a baby's cry. For months, mornings had been so quiet, then for weeks, there had been Michel Linteau's almost speech-like babblings. Now, in Marie-Claire's sleep-muddled mind, it was summer, Emilie was curled beside her in their bed, and Maman would be rising soon to feed Philippe.

When Marie-Claire opened her eyes, the space beside her in the bed was empty and cold. Patterns of frost were etched on the windows. The familiar claws of grief raked at her heart. The baby continued to cry.

When neither Tante Thérèse nor Maman appeared, Marie-Claire hurried across the cold floor and lifted Angélique from the cradle. The moment she did, the baby quieted, her eyes open wide. Marie-Claire smiled. It was hard to stay sad for long with a creature like this in the house.

"Are you surprised to see me?" Marie-Claire cooed. "Your maman is probably outside doing what I would say, from the feel of your soggy diaper, you have done right here. She will be back shortly," she continued, amused by how Angélique's eyes danced at the sound of her voice, "but would you like me to change you out of your wet things?"

Marie-Claire took a clean diaper from the small pile under the cradle. She laid Angélique on her bed, unfastened the pins, and dropped the heavy weight of wet cloth to the floor. Angélique waved her fists in the air and kicked her legs. Marie-Claire placed the fresh diaper under the baby's red little behind. "Such a pretty girl you are," she said. "And look how nice and fat you are growing."

Carefully Marie-Claire slipped her fingers between the diaper and the baby's skin as she jammed each pin through the thick flannel.

Tante Thérèse hurried in the door with a gust of cold wind, shaking snow from the bottom of her nightgown. "Thank you, Marie-Claire. If you would keep her a little longer, I will get some water heating on the stove so I can wash diapers this morning."

Tante Thérèse was filling the wash kettle and Marie-Claire was cradling Angélique in her arms when Maman emerged from her bedroom. Her tousled hair reminded Marie-Claire of the awful weeks after Emilie's passing, but recently Maman's spirits had been so much better. Picking up the soap carving from the table, Maman said, "Didn't this turn out beautifully? Laura is a lucky girl to be receiving such a gift."

With the angel tucked carefully in her pocket, Marie-Claire hurried through the streets. She hurried to keep herself warm and because Maman expected her help with the cooking that she and Tante Thérèse had been starting when Marie-Claire left. The family was preparing for the many gatherings that would take place between *Noël* and *le jour de l'An*.

When Marie-Claire reached Laura's neighbourhood, men in horse-drawn sleighs were delivering milk and bread right to the doors of the fine mansions. At the Waterfords' door, Marie-Claire took a deep breath and raised her hand to the big brass knocker.

"Bonjour," Céleste greeted her. "Come in quickly, Marie-Claire, out of the cold."

Marie-Claire was pleased that Céleste remembered her name. *"Bonjour,* Céleste. May I see Laura please? Is she at home?"

Up the grand staircase Céleste called, "You have a visitor, Laura. Shall I send her up to your room?"

"Yes, please."

Marie-Claire said, "With such wonderful smells coming from the kitchen, I thought Laura must be baking."

"Laura doesn't like to do kitchen chores," Céleste said. "But I'll bring you girls a plate of cookies shortly, shall I?"

"Oh, I did not mean—"

Céleste laughed. "Don't worry. I know you didn't. I can tell that your parents have brought you up well."

Laura closed the book she was reading and smiled. "Marie-Claire! I did not expect to see you again!"

"I bring *un cadeau* ... a present. For Christmas." Marie-Claire put her hand in her pocket. "I have no pretty paper to wrap, but here. I make it for you."

"What is it?"

Marie-Claire felt the smile fade from her face. *"C'est un ange,"* she said. "It is ... an angel. I make it."

"Oh, yes, I see." Laura ran a finger over the carving. "It's kind of bumpy."

Marie-Claire wanted suddenly to run from the room, angry and ashamed at the same time. How could Laura be so rude? And what had she, Marie-Claire, been thinking, bringing a gift to someone who had so many lovely things—a doll with real hair, a palace in a snowy little globe, a shiny white toilet.... What did she think such a person would want with a lumpy bit of soap?

"It is lovely, too. Thank you," Laura said quickly. She kissed Marie-Claire on the cheek. "I especially like her wings and her little halo."

Feeling somewhat reassured, Marie-Claire said, "A halo very little. I think she is not the most ... goodest of the angels." She giggled, nervous

"I have no pretty paper to wrap, but here. I make it for you," Marie-Claire said.

about her use of English and imagining what sort of naughtiness a small-haloed angel might get up to.

Laura giggled too, then turned the soap angel over in her hand. "I can't believe you made this yourself."

Marie-Claire's back straightened. "Yes, I made it! I—"

Laura assured her that she *did* believe her.

"But you say, '*I can't believe you.*' Does it not mean—?"

Laura shook her head. "It means only that I think you are very clever."

Sometimes trying to understand English was so confusing. But then, it was probably hard to learn any language well just by listening to people chatting in the streets and in the square.

"Say," Laura said, dropping the soap angel onto the bed, "Christmas is only two days away. Do you know what you're getting?"

"In my family, we give a gift at … *le jour de l'An.*"

"Not at Christmas?"

"No." Marie-Claire held her thumb, said, "Christmas," then counted with her fingers till she'd indicated enough days to make a week. Holding that finger she said, *"Le jour de l'An."*

Laura nodded, but Marie-Claire wasn't sure she'd really understood.

"I'm getting new skates," Laura said.

"How you know?"

"Because that's what I asked for."

Marie-Claire's mind reeled. Laura didn't help in the kitchen because she didn't like to. She had only to ask and she would receive whatever she wanted. And she thought nothing, it seemed, of receiving a gift bigger than would fit in a stocking. Marie-Claire had always been delighted by whatever little gift the Baby Jesus left her—an orange, a banana, or a piece of barley sugar in the shape of an animal. How lucky Laura was to be getting skates!

Marie-Claire was just figuring out how to say that she must be getting home when Laura's mother appeared in the doorway. "Hello," she said, looking down her long nose. To Laura she said, "I'm afraid it's time for the little French girl to be going." Briskly she disappeared.

Marie-Claire felt her face flush. Why did being sent home feel so awful when she was planning to go already? The way Mrs. Waterford spoke— no "How are you? How is your arm? I hope it is feeling better"—it almost seemed as if Marie-Claire were not welcome here. But why? *Time for "the little French girl" to be going.* Was it because she was French? Or did it just sound that way?

Maybe it was fine for a French person to come into this grand home to work, or if Mrs. Waterford were feeling guilty about her horse almost running you down. Just don't think about coming here on a friendly basis.

"You don't have to go right away," Laura said.

"Yes," Marie-Claire said, "I do."

In one way she wanted to stay with Laura and her lovely things all morning. In another, she could not get out of there quickly enough.

"Before I go," she asked—wanting to stay was winning the battle inside her—"may I see, one time, some snow on your little palace?"

Laura took from the shelf the snow globe Marie-Claire had so admired on her first visit, after the accident. Laura turned the globe upside down and upright again. Around the walls of the castle, sparkly flakes drifted down.

Never before had Marie-Claire's stomach hurt from wanting a *thing*—a mere object—so badly. She longed to just grab it from Laura's hands and run.

When the snow had settled, Laura handed the globe to Marie-Claire. For a flickering instant Marie-Claire thought Laura might be handing it to her to keep, as she had her nightgown.

"You do it this time," Laura said.

The globe was heavy in Marie-Claire's hands, like a pound of butter. Oh, how she wished, as she turned it over, that it were hers!

Immediately she scolded herself for thinking such a covetous thought. But she just couldn't help it. The miniature palace scene was magical, almost as good as the real thing. When the snow had settled for a second time, Marie-Claire forced herself to hand the globe back to Laura.

And Laura replaced it on the shelf.

CHAPTER N.º 5

*On the day before Christmas, Marie-*Claire sat in the back pew of the church, her head bowed. Which of her sins, she wondered, should she confess to the priest when her turn came? She had obeyed many of the Ten Commandments recently—honouring Maman and Papa, not using the Lord's name in vain. And she had certainly not killed anyone. But she had done less well with others—giving far more thought to the Ice Palace that she wanted so much to see built in the square again than to her prayers, for one thing. As for being vain and coveting her neighbour's belongings ... Marie-Claire sighed.

Wanting skates like those she'd seen people wearing on the river and at rinks seemed such a little sin now, with all she found herself wanting of late: a doll like the one Laura had; a snowy globe containing a little palace she could see and hold every day—even just one pretty dress like those hanging in Laura's wardrobe. Every time she went out in the cold to the outhouse, she remembered the shiny toilet right inside Laura's house and wished she had one of those, too. *And* a bathtub and basin with pipes full of wonderful hot water.

Marie-Claire pushed aside the red velvet curtain to the confessional, stepped inside the boxy little room, and knelt down before the blank wall. "Bless me, Father, for I have sinned. It has been three weeks since my last confession."

The priest slid back the panel in the wall between them, revealing only faintly his lined face in the pale light. "How have you sinned, my child?"

"I have coveted my neighbour's possessions. I think about the Ice Palace often. And, Father, one day I thought it would be fun to go on a toboggan slide."

"Are you truly sorry for your sins?"

"Yes, Father."

"Say five Hail Marys and you will be forgiven. And pray to God for holy thoughts."

Marie-Claire did as the priest said. Her heart lighter, she ran home to help Maman and Tante Thérèse prepare for the festivities soon to come. In spite of all they had already done, there was still pastry to roll, meat to grind for *tourtière,* and more biscuits to bake.

Maman gave Marie-Claire the job of whipping the cream for the special cake Papa so liked. Round and round in the heavy earthenware bowl, Marie-Claire flicked the whisk as fast as her arm would go. Her arm grew hot, and hotter, and more tired with every turn. When it felt as if it would fall off if she whisked a second longer, she simply *had* to take a rest. Her arm tingled as she let it dangle at her side.

But the cream looked just as thin as it had when she began. When she started to beat again, Maman said, "Keep the movement in your wrist. Remember, you are mixing two ingredients: the cream and the air."

Again Marie-Claire beat the cream, making good big but fast circles with the whisk. Gradually the cream began to thicken. She kept on beating, even as the muscles in her arm begged her to stop. Finally, when she again thought her arm would drop off if she tried to go on, the whipped cream began to form the pretty little peaks she was after. She put the bowl in the pantry, where it was cool enough in winter not to need ice in the icebox.

"May I lick the whisk and bowl, Maman?"

"Oui, ma chérie, certainement" Maman pulled a *tourtière* from the oven and put another stick in the wood stove.

Marie-Claire licked the whisk clean, then began to wipe the bowl with her finger. Other

Christmases, she and Emilie had kept a close eye on each other, making sure the other sister didn't get more than her share. Now that Marie-Claire could have all the bits of whipped cream for herself, they seemed, somehow, to taste not quite as special.

"Finished?" Maman said. "You might like to have a little sleep this afternoon. You will be up very late tonight."

"I'm not tired," Marie-Claire insisted. Who could sleep in the daytime anyway, right before the most wonderful night of the year?

"Well then," Maman said, "how would you like to take this little *tourtière* around to the widow Cornet? I invited her to join us tonight after mass, but she prefers to be alone. Poor dear, she has had a very hard year."

Marie-Claire smiled, proud that her maman, who had suffered such losses herself this year, was able to think of someone who had suffered more.

CHAPTER N° 6

Stars shone brightly in the crisp night sky.
The cold air was still. Excited to get to the church, Marie-Claire and Lucille walked ahead of their families.

Marie-Claire said to her cousin, "The white cloud of your breath is almost like a halo around your head." She began to sing one of her favourite hymns. *"Je suis aux anges ..."*

Lucille laughed. "You have too much imagination, Marie-Claire. An angel I am not! Today, watching people on a toboggan run, I actually longed to be hurtling down it with them!"

"Oh, Lucille! You too?"

The girls lowered their voices as they entered the doors of the church. Before heading up the long aisle to their seats, they each dipped a hand in holy water and made the sign of the cross as they genuflected before it. Marie-Claire wondered if Laura was at her own church tonight.

For a month this church had been undecorated. Now, on Christmas Eve, the altar was covered with a gold-embroidered cloth, and the sanctuary was adorned with gold ornaments, candles, and bright metal flowers. Quiet chat filled the pews, along with the smell of incense and damp wool—until a lone strong voice began to sing *Minuit, chrétiens*. Marie-Claire was sure, right from the opening note, that inside her chest, her heart was vibrating with the music.

The whole church seemed to hum with excitement as the hymn was sung. A tall clergyman dressed in a long red robe embroidered with gold slowly entered the church, carrying a gold statue of the Virgin Mary on his shoulder. Behind him another clergyman carried a cross. Following him, at least a dozen men carried torches. Then came the boys of the choir, some in black robes, some in red, followed by candle-holders dressed all in purple. Finally came the moment Marie-Claire always liked best.

Someone carried in *L'Enfant Jésus* and laid Him in the manger. All around the church, real babies cooed and burbled. Marie-Claire looked at Maman. Was she struck by the extra power in the arrival of *L'Enfant* this Christmas too?

Maman turned at that moment from Papa to Marie-Claire and smiled. Marie-Claire slipped her hand into Maman's and smiled back.

When the first angel arrived carrying a bright star and singing the high, clear notes of the *Gloria,* Marie-Claire thought her heart would break from the beauty. All of tonight's ceremony was so familiar, and yet different somehow, as if all that the Laroches had survived this year—along with so many families here—had somehow

41

made them even stronger and even more beloved children of God than they had been before.

After the shepherds arrived singing *Berger vois-tu là-bas,* to complete the tableau of the *crèche,* worshippers took communion, first the men and then the women. The choir sang more hymns, including Marie-Claire's favourites—*D'ou viens tu bergerer?, Il est né le divin enfant,* and *Les anges dans nos campagnes*—and she let the sweet strains of the music wash over her.

Louis gently shook Marie-Claire's shoulder. "Time to go home," he said, "for the wonderful meal you have been helping Maman and Tante Thérèse to prepare."

Marie-Claire rubbed her eyes. She must have dozed off during the long communion. "Lucille and her family are coming too, aren't they?"

"Of course."

Crunching home through the snow-clogged streets, Marie-Claire felt suddenly very hungry for *tourtière,* molasses biscuits, and special cake with whipped cream.

Late into the night, sounds of merriment filled the house as everyone celebrated Christmas. The baby, Angélique, slept peacefully through it all.

CHAPTER *N°* 7

In the days following, toboggans flashed down the steep streets of Montreal. Where snow was lumpy, they leapt into the air and landed with a thud. All the toboggan runs made of wood were up and operating now too.

After what the priests had said about the sinfulness of tobogganing—especially for women—Marie-Claire found it a little shocking to see many young women hurtling down the runs, their legs flung impolitely in the air, the arms of men wrapped so publicly around their middles. She could certainly not imagine Maman or Tante

Thérèse doing such a thing, or even Céleste, who clung to Louis's sleeve and laughed with delight at the tobogganers.

All the same, it was hard to understand why God would want to punish people for enjoying themselves in this way. A visiting priest had said that was why smallpox had come and taken so many lives, but it made no sense. Emilie and other children who had died had never ridden a toboggan. It made no sense at all.

Hundreds of people were out enjoying the sun that shone brilliantly on the fresh snow—people in long coats and hats of beaver, moose, and seal and in short, hooded coats of chestnut-coloured wool, their waists tightly wound with fringed belts. There were stylish women with large bustles under their skirts, too, but Marie-Claire could not imagine wanting to look as if her *derrière* stuck out such a long way behind her.

At one of the many rinks that Marie-Claire, Louis, and Céleste strolled past, skaters flew by, their skate-blades hissing.

"Come skate with us, Marie-Claire," Céleste said, as she and Louis stepped onto the ice in their boots.

Usually Marie-Claire was happy to slide in her boots, one foot pushing forward, then the other. But noticing so many little girls out with their families, and missing Emilie, she did not feel like it today. Maybe if she had skates, she would feel more like skating. But she didn't, so she wandered instead across the square and plunked herself down on a bench that faced the area where the Ice Palace would soon be built.

Louis and Céleste came up behind her, breathless. "The ice on the rink is very fast. Are you sure you don't want to slide?"

Marie-Claire kicked the heel of her boot into the hard-packed snow. "I wish I had skates."

"Maybe someday you will," Céleste said.

Someday. Marie-Claire shrugged. "At least there is one thing I can have soon."

"What is that?"

"The ice on the rink is very fast. Are you sure you don't want to slide?" asked Louis.

"Soon the Ice Palace will be shining here again like diamonds in the sun. Louis, do you think Maman will allow me to come and see it with you at night, as she did last year?"

A worried expression froze for a brief instant on Louis's face before he managed to hide it.

"What is it? Louis?"

"I am afraid, Marie-Claire, that the city has decided ... with all the disruption this year with smallpox ... it ..."

Céleste crouched down and folded her gloved hands around Marie-Claire's. "Your brother is trying to say that there will be no Ice Palace this year."

Louis began to explain why, but Marie-Claire did not care to hear. She did not want her brother's hand on her shoulder, trying to comfort her, or Céleste's sympathetic eyes upon her. She did not want the tears now stinging at the back of her own eyes. She began again to jab at the snow with her boot heel.

"Hello, Marie-Claire."

"Laura!"

"I have been watching you for a few minutes. You are sad today?"

Marie-Claire nodded. "A little." She did not feel like finding English words to explain but did not want to appear unfriendly. She smiled at Laura and noticed that the fur trim on her hat matched the muff into which Laura's hands were buried deep. Marie-Claire curled her own hands in tight balls inside her pockets.

"Can you come with me today to my house?" Laura said.

"Me?" She would be able to pee on that toilet again. Maybe Laura would again give her something, too. They could at least play together. They could be friends. But already feeling today like an old rag, could she bear to be around all of Laura's nice things? And—"Your mother? She ..."

"She won't mind. Please, come."

"May I, Louis?"

Marie-Claire was quick to notice that her soap carving stood small but proud on the night table beside Laura's bed.

"I love my little angel," the English girl said, picking it up. "I hold her every night when I'm saying my prayers."

Marie-Claire smiled, pleased to know that her gift was important to Laura. She was also pleased to know that Laura said prayers, even though she had no reminders of Jesus in her room.

Laura patted the space beside her on the edge of the bed. "Sit down, Marie-Claire. Tell me why you are sad."

"My brother, he say … this winter, there be no … *Palais de glace*."

"That's too bad. The palace last winter was wonderful, wasn't it?" Laura placed her angel back on the night table. "But there will be other ice sculptures. Are you sure there is not something else bothering you?"

Marie-Claire squeezed her eyes shut for a moment. "My sister," she said. "I miss her."

Laura sat back and stared at Marie-Claire. "I did not know you had a sister."

"I think I tell you. Maybe I tell Céleste."

"Where has your sister gone?"

Marie-Claire struggled to tell Laura about the black wagon that had come when she and Emilie had smallpox, how only she had come home from the hospital where they were taken. She used such a jumble of English and French words that she wasn't sure how much Laura understood. But when Marie-Claire looked up, tears were spilling onto Laura's cheeks.

Laura took a lace-edged handkerchief from her pocket and wiped her eyes. After a few moments, she crossed the room to the shelf, picked up the snow globe, and placed it in Marie-Claire's hands.

Sitting on Laura's bed, Marie-Claire watched

the magical snow drifting around the palace. Laura said, "I would like you to keep it."

Marie-Claire thought she must have misunderstood, but the English girl went on, "I have so much, you … Please, Marie-Claire, accept this, as a gift."

Her heart cried *Yes!* But she shook her head. She could not accept such a valuable gift. And yet, had she not badly wanted the snow globe every time she had seen it? "But you say before … your grandmother—"

"She gave it to me, yes, but it is mine to do with as I wish. And I wish to give it to you."

Wicked she might be for coveting her neighbour's possessions, but Marie-Claire was delighted, too, to again be the beneficiary of Laura's generosity.

Together, the girls sat watching the flurry of snowflakes in the glass ball that felt like gold in Marie-Claire's hands. The snow settled again, on and around the miniature palace. It truly was a beautiful thing.

Laura said, "Maybe having this will take away a little of your sadness about the real Ice Palace."

"Yes," Marie-Claire forced herself to say. "Thank you." The beautiful snow globe seemed to have become even more beautiful for having been given by someone who was beginning to feel—how strange—like a friend.

"First the nightgown, now this?" Maman, on her knees, wrung a wet rag over the bucket of water. "Is this what we have taught you is important?" She scrubbed a patch of floor, then sat back on her heels. "At least a person has *need* of a nightgown. But this … this *colifichet?*"

"It's just that … she likes me, Maman. And it's nice, that's all."

"Of course she likes you. What is not to like?" Maman resumed her scrubbing. Her hands were chapped and red. Wisps of hair clung to the perspiration at the side of her face. There was pride in the set of her jaw, even as she knelt by the bucket of dirty water.

"So, Maman," Marie-Claire said, "would you prefer that I return it?" She prayed that Maman would not say yes.

Maman rose from her knees, placed a hand in the small of her back, and straightened up. She picked up the bucket and took it outside to dump in the lane. When she came back inside, Marie-Claire, still holding the palace globe, said, "See, Maman, what happens when—?"

Without looking, Maman turned away to hang the wet rag by the wood stove. "Yes, I see."

Tears pricked the back of Marie-Claire's throat. She swallowed, set the globe on a windowsill, and said, "Where are my Tante Thérèse and Oncle Henri?"

"Thérèse and Henri are visiting some friends. Why? Are you hoping they will be more understanding? The problem is not with wanting something, Marie-Claire. The problem is becoming too attached to the idea of getting it."

Maman was right. Marie-Claire did hope her aunt and uncle would be more taken with the globe than Maman seemed to be. "I just wondered."

"Well, there is no time to stand around wondering. I need your help to get ready for tonight."

By the time everything was on the stove or in the oven and people began to arrive, Maman was all smiles—for Tante Celine, Oncle Marc, and Lucille and Bernadette, for the Flauberts from downstairs, and for the Linteau family, the widow Gaugin and her son, Georges, with whom the Linteaus were now living. Again and again she cheerfully cried, *"Entrez! Donnez-moi vos manteaux!"* And when Georges noticed the snow globe on the windowsill, and Marie-Claire explained where it had come from, Maman did not seem to be upset anymore about her having it.

All evening long—after the older children had received a gift of candy and each of the younger children a simple wooden toy—everyone ate and told stories. Everyone wanted to hear from Thérèse and Henri what Toronto was like.

"Muddy, but lots of good jobs," Henri said.

"It is a little lonely," Thérèse said quietly. "But we are here now!"

Monsieur Flaubert played his fiddle, and there was much singing and laughter. Marie-Claire, Lucille, and Georges took turns bouncing the Linteau children on their knees. Later, after the young children had fallen asleep on Marie-Claire's bed, the older girls held the babies and rocked them. Lucille whispered, "This morning I heard Maman tell Papa that she is to have a new baby next summer."

Marie-Claire gasped. "Perhaps," she whispered back, "you will get the brother you have wished for."

Amid much merriment, Lucille raised the Linteau baby to her shoulder and patted his back. Marie-Claire cuddled Angélique close, enjoying the warm weight of the little body against her arm and chest. To Lucille she said, "Just think, someday we will be sitting together like this with babies of our own."

"I am going to have twelve," Lucille said. "How many will you?"

Marie-Claire thought for a moment. "Six would be a nice number."

"Will you feed them with a bottle, do you think? Or—" Lucille lowered her voice "—the way Tante Thérèse does?"

"That way would be much easier," Marie-Claire said, "if I am lucky enough to have lots of milk."

Both girls were taken suddenly with a fit of giggles. When the baby at Lucille's shoulder let out a loud burp, they laughed even more. Once they were able to bring themselves under control, they joined in the singing with great exuberance.

At midnight, everyone paused in their festive celebrating to kneel, except Papa. As the oldest person there, it was his responsibility to give the benediction for the New Year. Above each person, he traced a cross in the air and said, *"Que le bon Dieu te bénisse comme je te bénis."*

Looking around the room and thinking about how all these people had been part of her life this year, and she of theirs, Marie-Claire felt an almost overwhelming pride. They had been through so much. All of them. But they were strong people. Even in the face of injury, disease, fire, and death, they carried on. And so did she. She was one of them. Strong and proud and ready to face together whatever the New Year brought.

Again, the music started up, and Marie-Claire remembered the scarf she had finally finished. She

"Just think, someday we will be together like this with babies of our own," Marie-Claire said to Lucille.

brought it out from under her bed and wrapped it around Papa's neck.

"*Merci beaucoup,* my clever daughter!" Papa gave Marie-Claire big kisses on both cheeks.

Monsieur Flaubert played more fiddle, and everyone sang on into the night.

Gradually the music slowed. The voices that filled the room grew softer. Angélique was heavy with sleep in Marie-Claire's arms. When Oncle Henri said, "Shall I put one more log in the wood stove?" everyone agreed that no, it was time to be getting home—time for bed.

The families who weren't staying gathered their coats. After they'd left, and after much in and out to the privy in the back lane, the Laroche family and Tante Thérèse, Oncle Henri, and Angélique settled in their beds.

Marie-Claire listened through the wall to the peaceful sound of her parents saying the rosary. She heard the rustling of bed covers that signalled their getting ready to sleep. Across the room Oncle Henri began to snore. Outside the window, the moon shone brightly. On the windowsill—she had all but forgotten it was there—sat the snow globe she had brought home from Laura's house that day. Or, yesterday it would be now, for they had stayed up very late. It had been such a good party.

CHAPTER N⁰ 9

The fire in the wood stove was crackling.
Outside the window, it was still dark. By the light
of a candle, Maman was quietly filling the kettle
from the bucket. Otherwise the house was still.

Marie-Claire watched Maman's familiar
movements. Something about them reminded
her of last night and how good it had felt to be
part of this family. Some mornings, it was she
herself who awoke early and did the chores
Maman was doing today. It felt good to know she
was as strong and as capable as Maman in similar
ways.

As Maman crossed the room toward the window, a little light from her candle caught the smooth glass of the snow globe on the sill and illuminated the castle inside. Marie-Claire lay as still as she could, not daring even to breathe, as Maman picked up the globe.

Maman shook it gently and watched the silvery snow swirling inside. "You are right, Marie-Claire, it is beautiful." So softly she spoke. She did not sound at all cross this morning.

"Yes," Marie-Claire whispered, wondering how Maman knew she was awake. "But I see—it makes you sad." She sat up, careful not to disturb Tante Thérèse. "Why?"

Maman sat on the edge of the already crowded bed. "A mother would like to be able to give her daughter all the beautiful things her heart might desire, whether she has need of them or not." She tucked a strand of Marie-Claire's hair behind her ear. "That's all."

Marie-Claire slipped her arms up inside Maman's shawl and hugged her fiercely.

"*A mother would like to be able to give her daughter all the beautiful things her heart might desire, whether she has need of them or not,*" Maman said.

"*Mon Dieu, ma fille!* So strong you are becoming!"

Marie-Claire looked up at Maman and smiled. The crinkly lines around her eyes, the silver strands in her dark hair, made her look quite beautiful in her own way. "We are strong people, Maman, eh?"

"Indeed we are. Tell me, strong daughter, would you like a cup of tea now, or would you like to stay in your bed for a little while?"

"Mmm … May I have a cup of tea in my bed?"

"*Quelle bonne idée, ma fille rusée!* Just be careful not to spill on your sleeping Tante Thérèse."

From the other side of the bed came a low, muffled voice. "You think I can sleep through all this chatter? How about a cup of tea for me too, Hélène?"

After breakfast, when the rest of the family was occupied, Marie-Claire wrapped the snow globe in a clean diaper, tucked it inside her coat, and said she was going out for some fresh air. When she had first seen the little treasure, she had wanted it more than anything she had ever wanted before—except to have her baby brothers and little sister back again. But Maman was right. She really did not need it, not like she needed a nightgown. Perhaps it would be enough to have seen it, to have held it, to know that such a thing existed. And to know that Maman agreed that it was a beautiful thing.

It *would* be enough, because she had seen the look in Maman's eyes even as she'd admired the lovely globe. Marie-Claire did not want anything so badly that she would be willing for Maman to be hurt every time she saw it.

Carrying her bundle carefully, she hurried through the quiet streets. It was too early for the tinsmith to be out, and shops on the main street were not yet open. The skating rink across from the square was empty. Facing the square where she had so often enjoyed remembering last year's Ice Palace, she sat down on a bench to rest.

It was where Laura had found her yesterday, before taking Marie-Claire to her beautiful home and giving her this generous gift. If she couldn't have the real palace, she could at least have this one. Marie-Claire felt proud of having made such a difficult decision. But perhaps … just one last look before returning it.

She removed the clean diaper in which the globe was wrapped. So smooth the cold glass. So magical the tiny flakes of snow drifting down through the water and settling on the little palace. Perhaps there was someplace other than the windowsill where she could keep it.

She was not going to keep it! How awful that her conviction to do the right thing could melt away so easily in the face of … what had Maman called it? *Un colifichet.* Before she confused herself further, Marie-Claire hurried up the hill to Laura's street.

CHAPTER № 10

*In the spacious entryway with the six-*flame chandelier overhead, Marie-Claire held out the snow globe to Laura. "I bring back."

"But ..." Laura looked quite shocked. "I want you to have it."

"I do not need it now," she said, thrusting it into Laura's hands. But she suddenly was not at all sure she believed the words she spoke. The snow globe wasn't like a nightgown, it was true, but was it possible to need something, if only for its beauty?

"It was a gift, Marie-Claire. It made me happy, giving it to you."

As it had made Marie-Claire happy to give Laura the soap angel, she realized.

"And after you took it home," Laura continued, "it made me happy knowing it was yours now and thinking how much you would be enjoying it."

Marie-Claire's mind reeled. How bad she would have felt if Laura had refused *her* gift of the soap angel! But how could she enjoy having the snow globe if it made Maman sad to see it? If she *didn't* keep it, though, she would be making *Laura* sad! And oh, the little palace in the globe truly was a beautiful thing. Even Maman, who was so very practical about everything, thought so. Maman ... *"Attend, je change d'avis!"*

"Pardon?"

Concentrating hard on her English, Marie-Claire said, "I would like ... accept *encore* ... your gift." She held out her hands. "May I?"

Smiling, Laura placed the globe back into Marie-Claire's hands. "I don't understand why you have changed your mind—again. But yes!"

"*Merci,* Laura. From Maman, also, *merci beau-coup.*"

"Excuse me? What has your mother to do with this?" Clearly, Laura was as confused now as Marie-Claire had been a few moments ago.

"If you not mind," Marie-Claire said, "I share ... your beautiful gift ... with her. Yes?"

"Oh yes! Yes!" Laura smiled.

"She has need of the beauty, too."

"Please, Marie-Claire, since you are here, will you stay and play with me for a little while?"

Marie-Claire did not want to appear ungrateful for the invitation, but Maman would be expecting her soon to help with chores, and later today Tante Thérèse, Oncle Henri, and Angélique would be going back to Toronto on the train. She wanted to spend as much time with them as possible before they left. She shook her head. "I'm sorry. I can't."

"Then promise to come back another day? Some time when your brother comes for Céleste, perhaps?"

Marie-Claire liked Laura but suspected deep down that they could never be real friends— visiting in each other's homes and sharing heartaches and joys in the special way she and Lucille so often did. She leaned forward and kissed Laura fondly on both cheeks. *"Au revoir."*

Turning to go, Marie-Claire peeked into the big room off the entrance hall where the Christmas tree stood. She glanced up the grand staircase where she had been carried, not nearly as long ago as it seemed. The snow globe she held would always be, for her, a reminder of the special experience she'd had here, in this place that few in her community would ever see. She hoped the snow globe would come to have a special, happy meaning for Maman too.

As the door closed behind her, Marie-Claire had a sudden impulse. An idea for one last gift to leave for Laura. Mrs. Waterford probably wouldn't like it, but Marie-Claire wouldn't worry about that. Chances were, she would never see her again.

Carefully she set her bundle on the edge of the driveway and stepped across the smooth white grounds to a spot she hoped Laura would be able to see from her bedroom. Snow worked its way into the tops of Marie-Claire's boots, but it didn't matter. She dropped to her back in the snow, then together and apart, together and apart, she swished her legs, at the same time as she slid her two arms up and down through the snow. There would be nothing lopsided about *this* angel. Carefully she made her way back to the driveway and retrieved her package.

When she reached the end of the driveway, Marie-Claire paused for a last look back at the mansion that, two weeks ago, she would never in all her life have expected to enter. Then she turned and looked out across the city that stretched from the heights of Mount Royal down to the St. Lawrence River.

Someone was out there, paddling a canoe among the ice floes. Above all the buildings, between the paddler and where Marie-Claire stood, towered the tall steeples of the city's many churches. She could also make out the dome of the building not far from the market where she and Maman shopped. She knew that her home was among those huddled cozily together nearby.

Down the hill Marie-Claire ran and along the main street. Once across St. Laurent, she slowed down. When she passed the square, she felt somehow older than she had when she had sat there, so recently, longing for the reappearance of the Ice Palace. Of course, why wouldn't she feel older? It was now 1886. She would soon be eleven years old!

A few people were out now in the narrow streets made even more narrow by heaps of snow. A scattering of children built snow forts on some corners, and in open spaces others made slides and snowmen. Overhead, the sky was heavy with the promise of more snow.

"Are those arms?" Marie-Claire asked a girl who was sticking chunks of snow to the sides of her snowman.

"Wings," the girl answered. "It is an angel."

Of course it was. Marie-Claire should know angel wings when she saw them! She smiled as she hurried on.

Beside the fire station was a skating rink she had not noticed before. Had she been daydreaming again, or had Papa forgotten to tell her, as he usually did, that the firemen had made a new one?

No one was skating on the rink this morning, perhaps because of the brisk wind—although cold didn't often keep Montrealers indoors. Perhaps many were still sleeping after all of last night's festivities.

Marie-Claire did not want to linger. But who in the whole world could resist having a skating rink all to herself? Again, she set the gift from Laura carefully in a safe place among chunks of snow.

As Marie-Claire stepped onto the ice, fresh snow began to fall in silvery flakes from the grey dome of sky above her.

Over the smooth surface she slid, one foot pushing forward, then the other. She glided up and down the length of the rink, sheltered from the wind by the wall of the fire station. She stepped off the ice and went to a spot from which she could take a good run at it.

She paused to examine the snowflakes landing on her dark sleeve. How different each one was, and yet each one was beautiful in its own way.

Marie-Claire ran hard to the edge of the ice, planted her feet firmly, raised her arms straight in the air, and slid—right up the middle of the ice as smooth as glass all the way to the far end. The snow drifted down in lacy clumps and settled on her woollen shoulders, on her eyelashes, and on the ice and streets around her.

Legs pushing, arms pumping, she headed back down the rink for one last skate. Then, after retrieving the treasure that would be hers and Maman's, it truly was time to be getting home.

And Marie-Claire couldn't wait to get there.

Dear Reader,

This has been the fourth and final book about Marie-Claire. We hope you've enjoyed meeting and getting to know her as much as we have enjoyed bringing her—and her wonderful story—to you.

Although Marie-Claire's tale is told, there are still eleven more terrific girls to read about, whose exciting adventures take place in Canada's past—girls just like you. So do keep on reading!

And please—don't forget to keep in touch! We love receiving your incredible letters telling us about your favourite stories and which girls you like best. And thank you for telling us about the stories you would like to read! There are so many remarkable stories in Canadian history. It seems that wherever we live, great stories live too, in our towns and cities, on our rivers and mountains. We hope that Our Canadian Girl captures the richness of that past.

Sincerely,
Barbara Berson

Canada's

1608
Samuel de Champlain establishes the first fortified trading post at Quebec.

1759
The British defeat the French in the Battle of the Plains of Abraham.

1812
The United States declares war against Canada.

1845
The expedition of Sir John Franklin to the Arctic ends when the ship is frozen in the pack ice; the fate of its crew remains a mystery.

1869
Louis Riel leads his Métis followers in the Red River Rebellion.

1871.
British Columbia joins Canada.

1755
The British expel the entire French population of Acadia (today's Maritime provinces), sending them into exile.

1776
The 13 Colonies revolt against Britain, and the Loyalists flee to Canada.

1837
Calling for responsible government, the Patriotes, following Louis-Joseph Papineau, rebel in Lower Canada; William Lyon Mackenzie leads the uprising in Upper Canada.

1867
New Brunswick, Nova Scotia and the United Province of Canada come together in Confederation to form the Dominion of Canada.

1870
Manitoba joins Canada. The Northwest Territories become an official territory of Canada.

1762
Elizabeth

Timeline

1885
At Craigellachie, British Columbia, the last spike is driven to complete the building of the Canadian Pacific Railway.

1898
The Yukon Territory becomes an official territory of Canada.

1914
Britain declares war on Germany, and Canada, because of its ties to Britain, is at war too.

1918
As a result of the Wartime Elections Act, the women of Canada are given the right to vote in federal elections.

1945
World War II ends conclusively with the dropping of atomic bombs on Hiroshima and Nagasaki.

1873
Prince Edward Island joins Canada.

1896
Gold is discovered on Bonanza Creek, a tributary of the Klondike River.

1905
Alberta and Saskatchewan join Canada.

1917
In the Halifax harbour, two ships collide, causing an explosion that leaves more than 1,600 dead and 9,000 injured.

1939
Canada declares war on Germany seven days after war is declared by Britain and France.

1949
Newfoundland, under the leadership of Joey Smallwood, joins Canada.

1897
Emily

1885
Marie-Claire

1939
Ellen